SHE DEVIL
(THE GIRL ON THE HELL SHIP)

BY

ROBERT E. HOWARD

British Library Cataloguing-in-Publication Data
A catalogue record for this book is available from the
British Library

Robert E. Howard

Robert Ervin Howard was born in Peaster, Texas in 1906. During his youth, his family moved between a variety of Texan boomtowns, and Howard – a bookish and somewhat introverted child – was steeped in the violent myths and legends of the Old South. Although he loved reading and learning, Howard developed a distinctly Texan, hardboiled outlook on the world. He became a passionate fan of boxing, taking it up at an amateur level, and from the age of nine began to write adventure tales of semi-historical bloodshed. In 1919, when Howard was thirteen, his family moved to the Central Texas hamlet of Cross Plains, where he would stay for the rest of his life.

At fifteen Howard began to read the pulp magazines of the day, and to write more seriously. The December 1922 issue of his high school newspaper featured two of his stories, 'Golden Hope Christmas' and 'West is West'. In 1924 he sold his first piece – a short caveman tale titled 'Spear and Fang' – for $16 to the not-yet-famous *Weird Tales* magazine. He published with the magazine regularly over the next few years. 1929 was a breakout year for Howard, in that the 23-year-old writer began to sell to other magazines, such as *Ghost Stories* and *Argosy*, both of whom had previously sent him hundreds of rejection slips. In 1930, he began a correspondence with weird fiction master H. P. Lovecraft which ran up to his death six years later, and is regarded as one of the great correspondence cycles in all of fantasy literature.

It was partly due to Lovecraft's encouragement that Howard created his most famous character, Conan the Cimmerian. Conan – a barbarian-turned-King during the Hyborian Age, a mythical period of some 12,000 years ago – featured in seventeen *Weird Tales* stories between 1933 and 1936, and is now regarded as having spawned the 'sword and sorcery' genre, making Howard's influence on fantasy literature comparable to that of J. R. R. Tolkien's. The Conan stories have since been adapted many times, most famously in the series of films starring Arnold Schwarzenegger.

Howard was enjoying an all-time high in sales by the beginning of 1936, but he was also deeply upset by the ill health of his mother, who had fallen into a coma. On the morning of June 11, 1936, he asked an attending nurse whether she would ever recover, and the nurse replied negatively. Howard walked to his car, parked outside the family home in Cross Plains, and shot himself. He died eight hours later, aged just thirty.

Outside, where dawn was just dispelling the fog-wisps from the South Pacific waters, the sea was calm, but a typhoon was raging in the cabin of the *Saucy Wench*. Most of the thunder was supplied by Captain Harrigan--vociferous oratory, charged with brimstone and sulphur, punctuated with resounding bangs of a hairy fist on the table across which he was bellowing damnation and destruction at Raquel O'Shane, who screamed back at him. Between them they were making so much noise they did not hear the sudden shouting that burst forth on deck.

"*Shut up!*" bawled the captain. He was broad as a door and his undershirt revealed a chest and arms muscled and hairy as an ape's. A growth of whiskers bristled his jaws, and his eyes blazed. He was a spectacle to daunt any woman, even if she had not known him as Bully Harrigan, smuggler, blackbirder, pearl-thief and pirate, when opportunity offered itself.

"Shut up!" he repeated. "One more yap out of you, you Spanish-Irish gutter-snipe, and I'll bend one on your jaw!"

Being a man of primal impulses, he demonstrated his meaning by a fervent swipe of a mallet-like fist, which Raquel dodged with the agility of much practice. She was slim and supple, with foamy black hair, dark eyes that blazed with deviltry, and an ivory-tinted skin, heritage of her mixed Celtic-Latin blood, that made men's heads swim at first sight. Her figure agitated by her movements, was a poem of breath-taking grace.

"Pig!" she screamed. "Don't you dare lay a finger on me!" This was purely rhetorical; Harrigan had laid a finger on her more than once during the past weeks, to say nothing of whole fists, belaying pins, and rope's ends. But she was still untamed.

She too banged the table and cursed in three languages.

"You've treated me like a dog all the way from Brisbane!" she raged. "Getting tired of me, are you, after taking me away from a good job in San Francisco--"

"I took you--" The enormity of the accusation choked the captain. "Why, you Barbary Coast hussy, the first time I ever saw you was that night you climbed aboard as we were pullin' out and begged me on your blasted knees to take you to sea and save you from the cops, account of your knifin' a Wop in that Water Street honky-tonk where you were workin', you--"

"Don't you call me that!" she shrieked, doing a war-dance. "All I did in that joint was dance! And I've played square with you, and now--"

"Now I'm sick of your tantrums," quoth Harrigan, downing a horse-sized snort from a square-faced bottle. "They're too much even for a good-hearted swab like me. As soon as we raise a civilized port, I'm goin' to kick you off onto the docks. And you give me any more lip, and I'll sell you to the first Kanaka chief I meet, you blasted hell-cat!"

That set her off again, like a match to the fuse of a sky-rocket. She hit the roof, and for a few moments the cabin was so full of impassioned feminine profanity it even drowned out Harrigan's roars.

"And where are we heading?" she demanded, remembering another grievance. "I want to know! The crew wants to know! You've told us nothing since we left Brisbane! We've picked up no cargo, and now we've gotten into these God-forsaken seas where none of us knows where we are, except you, and all you do is guzzle booze and study the blasted chart!"

She snatched it from the table and brandished it accusingly.

"Gimme that!" he bellowed, grabbing wildly. She jumped back agilely, sensing it was precious to him, and woman-like seizing the advantage.

"I won't! Not till you promise to quit knocking me around! Get back! I'll throw it out the port-hole if you come any closer!" Her rapid breathing, her agitation, made her loveliness devastating, but for the moment, he had no eyes for that.

With a frantic roar Harrigan lunged, upsetting the table with a crash. Raquel had raised a bigger hurricane than she had expected or intended. She squealed in alarm and leaped back, the chart waving wildly in her hand.

"Gimme that!" It was the howl of a lost soul. Harrigan's hair stood straight up and his eyes bulged. Raquel yelped with terror, too confused to make her peace by delivering the article requested. She sprang backward, tripped over a chair and fell on her back, with a shriek and an involuntary abandon that tossed her bare ivory-tinted legs revealingly skyward. But Harrigan was blind to this entrancing display. For as she fell, her arm, thrown out wildly, propelled the chart through the air; and as the Devil always controls such things, it sailed through the open port-hole.

Harrigan tore his hair and rushed for the port-hole. On deck an ear-splitting racket had burst suddenly forth but the occupants of the cabin ignored it. Harrigan, glaring pop-eyed from the port-hole, was just in time to see the chart vanish on its way to Davy Jones's locker, and his agonized howl paled all his previous efforts--so much so that out in the passageway the bos'n, who had just reached the cabin door in breathless haste, turned tail, and fled back the way he had come. Raquel had risen, in apprehensive silence, and was making some necessary adjustments in her garments. Her lovely eyes dilated at the red glare in Harrigan's eyes as he wheeled toward her.

"You threw that away on purpose!" he choked. "A million dollars right through the damn port-hole! I'll fix you--"

He lunged and she skipped back with a squeal, but not quickly enough. His huge paw closed on a shoulder-strap. There was a shriek, a ripping sound, and Raquel fled toward the door minus the dress which remained in Harrigan's hand. He was after her instantly, but panic winged her small feet. She beat him to the door and slammed it in his face, and even tried to hold it against him until convinced of her folly by a big fist which, crashing through the panels, grazed her dainty nose, filling her eyes with stars and tears. She yipped pitifully, abandoned the door, and fled up the companion-way, a startling figure in slippers and pink chemise.

After her came Captain Harrigan, a bellowing, red-eyed, hairy monstrosity whose only passion was to sweep the deck from poop to forecastle with that supple, half-naked body.

In their different emotions of fright and fury they were not, even then, aware of the clamor going on upon the deck, until they came full on a scene so unique it even checked Harrigan short in his tracks.

Not so Raquel; she scampered across the deck, unnoticed by the mob milling in the waist, and sprang into the main shrouds before she turned and stared at the spectacle which had halted Harrigan.

7

Hemmed in by a ring of blaspheming seamen the mate, Buck Richardson, was locked in combat with a stranger whose breeches (his only garment) dripped sea-water. That Mr. Richardson should be battling a stranger was not unique; what was unique was that Mr. Richardson, the terror of a thousand ports, bucko deluxe and hazer extraordinary, was getting the prime essence of hell beaten out of him. His opponent was as big as he--a broad-shouldered, clean-waisted, heavy-armed man with wetly plastered black hair, blue eyes that blazed with the joy of mayhem, and lips that grinned savagely even when, as now, they were smeared with blood.

He fought with gusto that horrified even his hard-boiled audience. Continually he plunged in, head down, not blindly like a bull, but with his eyes open--except the one the mate had closed--hammering the luckless bucko like a blacksmith pounding an anvil. Richardson was bleeding like a stuck pig, and spitting pieces of broken teeth. He was blowing like a porpoise and in his one good eye there was a desperate gleam.

"Who's that?" demanded Harrigan aghast. "Where'd he come from?"

"We sighted him just as the fog lifted," said the bos'n, spitting carefully to leeward. "He was driftin' along in a open boat, balin' and cussin' somethin' fierce. His boat sunk under him before he could get it to the ship, and he swum for it. A shark tried to scoff him on the way, but he kicked its brains out or bit it in the neck, or done somethin' atrocious to it. That's Wild Bill Clanton!"

"The hell it is!" grunted the captain, staring with new interest. Then he swore as Clanton bashed Mr. Richardson on the snout with appalling results. "They're bleedin' all over my clean deck!"

"Well," said the bos'n, "as soon as he clumb over the rail he seen the mate and went for him. From the remarks they passed before they was too winded to cuss, I gathered that Buck stole a gal from Clanton once. I went after you, but you seemed busy, so I just let 'em fight."

Bam! Mr. Clanton's left mauler met Mr. Richardson's midriff with an impact that sounded like the smack of a loose boom against a wet sail. Bam! A mallet-like right-hander to the jaw and Mr. Richardson went reeling backward and brought up against the rail with a crack that would have fractured the skull of anybody except a bucko mate on a trading schooner.

Clanton went for him with a blood-thirsty yell--then his eyes encountered Raquel, poised in the ratlines. He stopped short, batted his eyes, his mouth wide open as he glared wildly at the ivory-tinted vision posed against the blue, in a sheer wisp of pink silk that tempted even as it concealed little.

"Holy saints of Hell!" breathed Clanton in awe--and at this instant Mr. Richardson, a bloody ruin, lurched away from the rail with a belaying pin. Bam! It crashed on Clanton's head and that warrior bit the deck. Mr. Richardson croaked gratefully and bestowed himself lovingly on his victim's bosom, naively intent on beating his brains out with his trusty belaying pin. But Clanton anticipated his design by drawing up his legs, after the manner of a panther fighting on its back, and, receiving the hurtling mate on his feet and knees, he catapulted Mr. Richardson over his head.

The mate smote the deck headfirst and reverberantly, and this time the impact was too much even for his adamantine skull. But Clanton, bounding up, observed some faint signs of life still, and sought to correct this oversight by leaping ardently and with both feet on the mate's bosom.

"Grab him!" yelled Harrigan. "He's killin' the mate!"

As no spectacle could have pleased the crew better than Mr. Richardson's violent demise, they made no move to obey. Harrigan ran forward blasphemously and tugging forth an enormous revolver thrust it under the nose of Mr. Clanton who eyed it and its owner without favor.

"Are you the cap'n of this mud-scow?" Clanton demanded.

"I am, by God!" gnashed Mr. Harrigan. "I'm Bully Harrigan! What are you doin' on board my ship?"

"I've been keepin' a damned sieve of a boat afloat for a day and a night," retorted the other. "I was mate aboard the *Damnation*, out of Bristol. The cap'n didn't like Americans. After I won his share of the cargo at draw poker, he welshed and put me afloat--with the aid of the crew."

Harrigan broodingly visualized the battle that must have required!

"Carry the mate to his bunk and bring him to," he ordered the men. "And for you, Clanton, you'll work for your passage! Get for'ard!"

Clanton ignored the command. He was again staring at the vision clinging to the ratlines. Raquel peeped at him approvingly, noting the clean-cut muscular symmetry that was his.

"Who's that?" he inquired, and all turned to stare. Harrigan roared like a sea-lion with awakened memory.

"Drag her down!" he yelled. "Tie her to the mast! I'll--"

"Don't touch me!" shrieked Raquel. I'll jump and drown myself!"

She didn't mean that, but she sounded as though she did. Clanton reached the rail with a tigerish bound, caught her wrist, and whipped her down onto the deck before she knew what was happening.

"Oh!" she gasped, staring at him with dilated eyes. He was bronzed by the sun of the Seven Seas, and his torso was ridged with clean hard cords of muscles. In fierce admiration his gaze devoured her from her trim ankles to the foamy burnished mass of her hair.

"Good work, Clanton!" roared Harrigan, striding forward. "Hold her!" Raquel wailed despairfully, but Harrigan, reaching for her, had his hand knocked aside, and he paused and goggled stupidly at Clanton.

"Avast!" roared Clanton gustily. "That's no way to treat a lady!"

"Lady, hell!" bleated Harrigan. "Do you know what she just did? Threw away my chart! The only dash-blank chart in the world that could show me how to find the island of Aragoa!"

"Was we goin' there, cap'n?" asked the bos'n.

"Yes, we was!" yelled Harrigan. "And what for? I'll tell you! Ambegis. A barrel full! At thirty-two dollars an ounce! You bilge-rats been grousin' to know where we were sailin' to--all right, I'll tell you! And then I'm goin' to tie that wench up and skin her stern with a rope's end!

"A few months ago a blackbirder bound for Australia went on a reef in a storm, off a desert island, and nobody but the mate got ashore alive. They'd found a mess of the stuff floatin' on the water, and filled a big barrel with it--and it floated ashore with him. The mate stood the solitude of the island as long as he could, and then took to sea in the ship's boat he'd patched up. He'd salvaged a chart and marked the island's position. He'd been weeks at sea when I picked him up, on my last voyage from Honolulu to Brisbane. He was ravin' and let slip about the ambergris--I mean he was that grateful to me for savin' him he told me all about it, and gimme the chart for safekeepin', and right after that he got delirious and fell overboard and drowned--"

Somebody laughed sardonically and Harrigan glared murderously around.

"He called the island Aragoa," he growled. "It ain't on no other chart. And now that the daughter of Jezebel has fed that chart to the sharks--"

"Why, hell!" quoth Clanton. "Is that all? Why, I can steer you to Aragoa without any blasted chart! I've been there a dozen times!"

Harrigan started and looked at him searchingly.

"Are you lyin'?"

"Belay with those insults!" said Clanton heatedly. "I won't take you anywhere unless you promise not to punish the girl."

"All right," snarled Harrigan, and Raquel sighed in relief. "But!" brandishing his gun in Clanton's face, "if you're lyin', I'll feed you to the sharks! Take the wheel and lay a course for Aragoa. You don't leave the poop till we raise land!"

"I've got to have food," growled Clanton.

"Tell it to the cook. Then get hold of that wheel." Reminded suddenly of Raquel's lightly-clad condition he roared: "Get below and get some clothes on, you shameless slut!"

A heavy toe emphasized the command by a direct hit astern, and she fled squeaking for the companion.

Clanton scowled, descended into the galley, and bullied the Chinese cook into setting out a feed that would have taxed the capacity of a horse. Having disposed of this, he swaggered up the poop ladder and took the wheel. The men watched him with interest, which was shared by Raquel, peeping from the companion. She had heard of him: who in the South Seas had not? A wild adventurer roaring on a turbulent career that included everything from pearl-diving to piracy, he was a man at least, not a beast like Harrigan.

Her flesh tingled deliciously with the feel of his strong grasp on her rounded arm; she was consumed with eagerness for more intimate contact with him, but the opportunity did not come until night had fallen and the powerful figure stood in solitary grandeur at the wheel.

His shoulders bulked against the South Sea stars as he held the schooner to her course; he might have posed for the image of intrepid exploration until a slender figure glided up the poop ladder.

"Does Harrigan know you're out here?" he demanded.

"He sleeps like a pig," she answered, her great dark eyes sad and wistful in the starlight. "He *is* a pig." She whimpered a little and leaned against him as if seeking pity and protection.

"Poor kid," he said with grand compassion, slipping a protecting arm about her waist--the paternal effect of which was somewhat marred by his patting of the swelling slope of a firm hip. A luxurious shudder ran through her supple body and she snuggled closer within the bend of his muscular arm and pressed her cheek against his shoulder.

"What did Harrigan say was the name of that island?" he asked.

"Aragoa!" she jerked her head back and stared at him, startled. "I thought you said you knew about it!"

"Never heard of it!" he declared. "I just said that to save you!"

"Oh!" she stood aghast. "What will we do when he finds out you lied?"

"I dunno," he answered. "We're in a jam that requires thought and concentration. Sneak down and steal me a few bottles of Harrigan's booze."

She cast him an uncertain glance, but moved away down the ladder, softly as an ivory-hued shadow, to return presently with an arm-ful of darkly gleaming bottles that made Clanton's eyes glisten. He lashed the wheel, casually sighting at a star on the horizon, and sat down by the rail.

"Set 'em down here," he requested, and when she complied, he grabbed her before she could straighten and pulled her down on his lap. For convention's sake she struggled faintly for a moment, and then her arms went convulsively around his corded neck, and she gave him her full red lips in a kiss that he felt clear to the tips of his toes.

"Judas!" During the entire course of a roving life he had never encountered a human volcano like this before. He shook his head to clear the swimming brain, took a deep breath and dived. When he came up for air, she was gasping too, quivering from the dynamic impact of his kisses.

Contentedly he knocked the neck off the bottle, took a deep swig and held it to her lips. She merely sipped; the night was still young, and she needed no alcoholic stimulant to drive the hot blood racing through her veins. It was already breaking all speed records.

Clanton did not need any stimulants either; but drank because he was thirsty; because liquor was to him what moonlight and perfume are to some men. At each swig he gulped as though he were trying to see the bottom.

By the time he had tossed an empty overboard he was saying: "To hell with Harrigan! If he gets gay with me, I'll kick his teeth out! I don't believe there's any such damn' place as Aragoa, anyway!"

"Who cares?" she breathed, leaning her supple back against his breast, and lifting her arms up and back to encircle his brawny neck. He ran an appreciative hand over a warm, rounded shoulder, and let his other hand rest on a knee.

Just as grey dawn stole over the sea, a terrific shock ran through the *Saucy Wench*. There was a crash in the galley, blasphemy in the forecastle, as men fell out of their bunks. The schooner lurched drunkenly--and remained motionless, with a list to starboard. Preceded by a blue-streaked haze of profanity Harrigan came hurtling from the companion and pranced up the poop ladder in his drawers.

"What the blitherin' hell?" he screamed. "My God, we're aground!"

From a litter of empty bottles Clanton rose unsteadily, stretched, yawned, spat and stared appreciatively at the jungle-fringed beach which--with only a narrow strip of shallow water between--stretched away from under the port bow.

"There's your island, Bully!" he announced with a magnificent gesture.

Harrigan tore his hair and howled like a wolf. "Did you have to run her onto the beach, you son of a slut?"

"That could have happened to anybody," asserted Clanton, and added reprovingly: "Where's your pants?"

But the captain had seen the broken bottles, and his howl had all the poignancy of a stricken soul. Then he saw something else. Raquel, awakened by the noise, rose uncertainly, rubbing her eyes childishly. She made a face, tasting again all the square-face she had guzzled the night before.

Harrigan turned purple; his arm windmilled, to the fascination of the crew who watched from the deck below. He found words, lurid and frenetic.

"You stole my liquor!" he roared. "You had my girl here all night! You've run my ship aground, and by God, I'm goin' to kill you, ambergris or no ambergris!"

He reached for his gun, only to discover that he wore neither gun nor belt. Bellowing he snatched a belaying pin from the rail and made at Clanton who smote him with such effect that the captain's head fractured the binnacle as his whole body performed a parabola backward.

At this moment a frightful figure appeared at the head of the starboard ladder--Mr. Richardson, bedecked in bandages, and with one good eye gleaming eerily. Not even such a beating as he'd received yesterday could long keep a true bucko in his bunk. In his hand was a revolver, and this he fired point-blank. But Mr. Richardson's one good eye was bleared, and his aim was not good. His bullet merely burned a welt across Clanton's ribs, and before he could fire again, Clanton's foot, striking his breastbone with great violence, catapulted him headlong down the ladder at the foot of which his head again met the deck with a force that rendered him temporarily *hors-de-combat.*

But Captain Harrigan had seized the opportunity to flee down the port ladder yelling: "Gimme my gun! I'll shoot 'em both!"

"Overboard!" yelled Clanton to Raquel, and then as she hesitated, he grabbed her around the waist, tossed her over the rail, and leaped after her.

The plunge into the water snapped her out of her hangover; she screamed, gasped, and then struck out for the beach, followed by Clanton. They reached it just as Harrigan appeared on the poop with a triumphant howl and a Winchester, with which he opened up on them as they raced across the sands and dived into the trees.

Under cover Clanton paused and looked back. The antics of Harrigan on the poop moved him to hearty guffaws, smiting his dripping thigh. Raquel glared at him, wringing out her skirt, and raking back a wet strand of hair.

"What's so funny about being marooned?" she demanded angrily.

He spanked her jocosely and replied: "Don't worry, kid. When the schooner sails, we'll be on her. You stay here and watch 'em while I go inland and look for fruit and fresh water. She's not stuck bad; they can warp her off."

"All right." She shucked her wet dress and hung it up to dry, while she lay down on her stomach on the soft dry sand to peer through the bushes at the ship. She made an alluring picture thus, her pink chemise dripping from their submersion, fitting her tighter than a glove. Clanton admired the view for a moment, and then departed through the trees, striding lightly and softly for so big a man.

Raquel lay there, watching the men piling into boats, with hawsers, where presently they were employed in yanking the schooner loose, stern-first, by main strength and profanity. But it was slow work. The sun rose, and Raquel got impatient. She was hungry and very, very thirsty.

She donned her dress, now dry, and started out to look for Clanton. The trees were denser than she had thought, and she soon lost sight of the beach. Presently she had to climb over a big log, and when she leaped down on the other side, a bramble bush caught up her skirt, twisting it high about her ivory thighs. She twisted about in vain, unable to reach the clinging branch or to free her skirt.

As she squirmed and swore, a light step sounded behind her, and without looking around she commanded, "Bill, untangle me!"

Obligingly a firm masculine hand grasped her skirt and freed it from the branch, by the simple process of raising it several inches. But her rescuer did not then lower the garment; indeed Raquel felt him pull it up even higher-- much higher!

"Quit clowning," she requested, turning her head--and then she opened her lovely mouth to its widest extent and emitted a yell that startled the birds in the trees. The man who was holding her skirt in such an indelicate position was not Clanton. He was a big Kanaka in breech-clout. Raquel made a convulsive effort to escape, but a big brown arm encircled her supple waist. In an instant the peaceful glade was a hurricane-center, punctuated by lusty shrieks that a big hand clapped over red-lipped mouth could not altogether stifle.

Clanton heard those screams as he glided like a big bronzed tiger toward the beach. They acted on him like a jolt of electricity. The next instant he was in full career through the jungle, leaving behind him a sizzling wake of profanity. Crashing through the bushes, he burst full onto a scene, striking in its primitive simplicity.

Raquel was defending her virtue as vigorously as civilized nations defend mythical possessions. Her dress had been torn half off and her white body and limbs contrasted vividly with the brown skin of her captor. He wasn't all brown, though; he was red in spots, for she had bitten him freely. So much so that irritation entered into his ardor, and, momentarily abandoning his efforts to subdue her by more pleasant means, he drew back an enormous fist for a clout calculated to waft her into dreamland.

It was at this moment that Clanton arrived on the scene and his bare foot, describing a terrific arc, caught the Kanaka under his haunches and somersaulted him clear over his captive, who scurried to her protector on her all-fours.

"Didn't I tell you to stay on the beach?" *Wham!* In his irritation Clanton emphasized his reproof with a resounding, open-handed slap where he could reach her easiest. Raquel's shriek was drowned in a vengeful roar. The Kanaka had regained his feet and was bounding toward them, swinging a knotty-headed war club he had leaned against a tree when he stole up on Raquel.

He lunged with a yell and a swing that would have spattered Clanton's brains all over the glade if it had landed. But it flailed empty air as Clanton left his feet in a headlong dive that carried him under the swipe and crashed his shoulders against the Kanaka's legs. Bam! They hit the earth together and the club flew out of the native's hand.

The next instant they were rolling all over the glade in a desperate dog-fight, gouging and slugging. Then Clanton, in the midst of their frantic revolutions, perceived that Raquel had secured the club and was dancing about, trying to get a swipe at his antagonist. Clanton, knowing the average accuracy of a woman's aim, was horrified. The Kanaka had him by the throat, trying to drive thumbs and fingers through the thick cords of muscle that protected the white man's wind-pipe and jugular, but it was the risk of being accidentally brained by a wild swipe of Raquel's club that galvanized Clanton to more desperate energy.

Fighting for an instant's purchase, he drove his knee into the Kanaka's groin, and the man gasped and doubled convulsively. Clanton broke away, kicking him heavily in the belly. Surprisingly the warrior gave a maddened yell, grabbed the foot and twisted it savagely. Clanton whirled to save himself a broken leg, and fell to his all-fours. At the same moment Raquel swung the too-heavy club. She missed as the Kanaka ducked, and she sprawled on her belly in the sand. Both men gained their feet simultaneously, but the Kanaka reached for the club. As he bent over Clanton swung his right over-hand like a hammer and with about the same effect. It crashed behind the Kanaka's ear with the impact of a caulking maul. The Kanaka stretched out in the sand without a quiver.

Raquel leaped up and threw herself hysterically in Clanton's arms. He shook her loose, with lurid language.

"No time for a pettin' party! There's a whole village of the illegitimates over toward the other side of the island. I saw it! Come on!" He grabbed her wrist and fled toward the beach with her, panting: "Thick brush, men cussin' on the ship. They wouldn't hear the racket we've made--I hope." She didn't ask why. She clutched her tattered dress about her as she ran.

They burst onto the beach, and saw that the *Saucy Wench* was afloat; she was anchored in clear water off the shore, and Harrigan was oiling his rifle on the poop, with the be-bandaged Richardson beside him.

"Ahoy!" yelled Clanton from behind a tree. "Harrigan! I've found your ambergris!"

Harrigan started violently and glared, head-down like a surly bear.

"What's that? Where are you? Show yourself!"

"And get shot? Like hell! But I'll make a trade with you. I've hidden the stuff where you'll never find it. But I'll lead you to it if you'll promise to take us aboard and put us ashore at some civilized port!"

"You fool!" whispered Raquel, kicking his shins. "He'll promise anything, and then shoot us when he's got the loot!"

But Harrigan was bellowing back across the strip of blue water.

"All right! Let bygones be bygones! I'm comin' ashore!"

A few moments later a boat was making for the beach. Raquel danced in her nervousness; her torn dress revealed flashing expanses of ivory flesh.

"Are you crazy? They'll kill us! And that native you knocked out will come to and get his tribe and--"

He grinned and stepped out on the beach, pulling her with him.

"They won't shoot us till I show them the ambergris! I'll take Harrigan inland; you wait here at the boat. And let me do the talkin'!"

She was not in the habit of meekly taking orders, but she lapsed into sulky and bewildered silence. She was badly scared.

Harrigan and Richardson piled out before the boat grounded. The captain had a Winchester, the mate a shotgun. They covered Clanton instantly.

"Stay here!" the captain told the half dozen men who had rowed him ashore. "Now then, Clanton, lead us to that ambergris, and no tricks!"

"Follow me!" Clanton led them into the jungle while behind at the boat, Raquel watched with dilated eyes and crawling flesh.

Clanton swung wide of the glade where--he hoped--the Kanaka still lay senseless. Hardly out of sight of the beach he stumbled over a root and fell. Sitting up he groaned, cursed and tenderly felt of his ankle.

"Blast the luck! It's broken! You'll have to rig a stretcher and carry me!"

"Carry you, hell!!" snorted Harrigan. "Tell us where the loot is, and we'll go on and find it ourselves."

"Go straight on about three hundred yards." groaned Clanton. "Till you come to a clump of sago-palms. Then turn to the left and go on till you come to a pool of fresh water. I rolled the barrel in there."

"All right," grunted Harrigan. "And if we don't find it, we'll shoot you when we get back."

"And we're goin' to shoot you whether we find it or not!" snarled Richardson. "That's why we left the men on the beach--didn't want no witnesses! And we're goin' to leave that wench to starve here with your skeleton when we sail. How you like *that*, huh?"

Clanton registered horrified despair, and both men chortled brutally as they strode away. They vanished among the trees, and Clanton waited a minute--five--ten--then he sprang up and sprinted for the beach.

He burst onto the beach so suddenly the bos'n nearly shot him.

"Pile in and row for the ship, Quick!" he yelled. "Cannibals! They've got Harrigan and the mate! Listen!"

Back in the jungle rose a sudden bedlam of shots and blood-freezing yells. It was enough. No heroic soul proposed a rescuing sortie. In another instant the boat was scudding for the schooner. Its occupants swarmed up the side, spurred by the rising clamor that was approaching through the jungle. Clanton stood on the poop and yelled orders, and they were obeyed without question.

The anchor came up with a rush, and the *Saucy Wench* was standing out to sea by the time the tribesman danced out on the beach. They swarmed to the water's edge, three or four hundred of them, yelling vengefully. One waved a blood-splashed shotgun, another a broken Winchester.

Clanton grinned; the directions he had given his enemies had led them accurately--straight into the native village! He thumbed his nose at the baffled barbarians on the beach, and turned and addressed the crew.

"As the only man aboard who can navigate, and owner of the ship, I'm assuming the position of cap'n! Do I hear any objections?"

The bos'n demanded: "What you mean, owner of ship?"

"Me and Harrigan matched pennies," asserted Clanton. "My share of the ambergris against the ship. I won."

"What about the ambergris?" demanded a hardy soul.

Clanton nodded back toward the receding beach. "Anybody that wants to swim back there and fight those boys for it, is welcome to try!"

In the self-conscious silence that followed, he barked suddenly: "All right, get to work! Tail onto those lines! There's a breeze makin' and we're headin' for the Solomons for a load of niggers for Queensland!"

As the crew jumped briskly, Raquel nudged him.

"You didn't find that ambergris," she said, her eyes ablaze with admiration. "That wasn't even the right island. That was all a lie!"

"I doubt if there ever was any ambergris," quoth he. "The fellow that made that chart was probably crazy. To hell with it!" He patted her plump hip possessively and added: "I reckon you go with the ship; that bein' the case I want to see you down in the cap'n's cabin, right away!"

THE END